- HERGÉ -
★

THE ADVENTURES OF TINTIN

THE CRAB WITH THE GOLDEN CLAWS

Little, Brown and Company
New York   Boston

www.casterman.com
www.tintin.com

Little, Brown and Company
Hachette Book Group
237 Park Avenue, New York, NY 10017
Visit our website at www.lb-kids.com

First Edition: April 2012

ISBN: 978-0-316-19876-9
2011921034
SC
Printed in China

Tintin and Snowy

It doesn't take much for Tintin and Snowy to start an adventure.
An old tin can is their first clue to this mystery!

Thomson

It may seem impossible to tell the clumsy police detectives apart.
But there is a secret way to separate Thomson from his partner—
look at their mustaches!

Thompson

Even though the two detectives dress identically, Thompson's mustache
droops downward, while Thomson's curls up at the ends!

Bunji Kuraki

This Japanese policeman has a letter for Tintin—
but he gets kidnapped before he can deliver it.

Allan

Crooked Allan is the first mate on board a ship named the *Karaboudjan*.
Allan lets a gang of smugglers use the ship for their villainous deeds.

Lieutenant Delcourt

Lieutenant Delcourt is in command of a remote outpost in the Sahara Desert.
His men rescue Tintin and Captain Haddock after an airplane crash.

Omar Ben Salaad

Omar Ben Salaad's big business in the city of Bagghar is just a front for his criminal smuggling activities.

THE CRAB
WITH
THE GOLDEN CLAWS

You've been lucky! You could have cut yourself. Look how jagged the edges are.

Now, come on! . . . And don't do that again, or I'll buy a muzzle and you'll walk on a lead!

Hi! Hello there, Tintin!

OLYMPIA BA

Waiter, bring another drink!

Yes, sir.

My dear Tintin, how nice to see you again! . . .

To be precise: how nice to see you again, my dear Tintin!

Here you are, sir.

Your health!

And yours!

My dear old friends, how nice to see you again!

Well, now, what's going on?

Everything's fine: we've just been entrusted with a very important case.

Oh?...

To be precise: a very ...er... important case.

Oh?...

Look... Have you read this?

"Watch out for counterfeit coins!" ...Yes, I saw it.

Well, we two have been instructed to clear this thing up.

Oh?... Jolly good!... I say, is it easy to spot one of these fakes?

Oh, you know how it is. People like ourselves who have examined them can tell one in a flash, of course...

Waiter!... How much?

Forty-five pence, sir.

Here's fifty pence!... But most people are easily fooled by them.

I'm sorry, sir...

Good gracious, someone's slipped me a dud fifty-pence piece!

CLUNK

There!

Thank you.

If you've nothing better to do, come along with us. We'll show you the papers we've already collected in our investigations.

Thanks.

Where did you put those papers?

But you put them away yourself!

!

What's that?

That? . . . It all came from Police Headquarters. They are things taken from a body found in the sea. Did you notice? He had five coins on him, all duds . . . Odd, don't you think?

Very odd! . . . May I . . . ?

I'll be back in a minute!

? ?

I'm going after him!

What's bitten him!

Good gracious! I've forgotten my stick!

Good gracious! He's forgotten his stick!

There he is!

We've caught him up.

What on earth's the matter?...

Well, the scrap of paper among those things found on the drowned man comes from the label off a tin ...

... and I was holding the very tin from which it was torn, just before I met you! Here we are. I threw it into that dustbin ... that one where the tramp is rummaging.

Tintin!... Aren't you ashamed of yourself? Rummaging in dustbins like a common mongrel off the streets!

One moment, please ...

It's gone!... Yet I'm sure I threw it there. A tin of crab, I remember quite clearly.

Open your sack!

No, it's not here ...

That's odd; in fact, it's fishy.

To be precise: it's fishy ...

What's all the fuss about?

Those chaps are absolutely daft! They are looking for an empty tin! A crab tin ...

A crab tin! Are they indeed!

Now, let's have a good look at this bit of paper...

Aha! That's interesting! There's something written here in pencil, almost obliterated by the water...

I must look at this through a magnifying glass.

Gnawing a bone again? Where did this one come from?...

Can't you ever do as you're told?

There!...And mind you don't do it again!

Did I leave it in my study?...

It's not here either!

CRASH

Crumbs! That made me jump . . . And it was only the wind slamming the door!

But now I think of it, that bit of paper . . .

. . . must have been blown away when I went into my study the first time to get my magnifying glass!

That's the answer. There it is!

Now let's have a look . . .

Have I gone crazy? I'm positive I put my magnifying glass down here a moment ago!

I'll go over all this in pencil. There's 'K' . . . and an 'A' . . . and that's an 'R' . . . or an 'I' . . . there, I'll soon have it . . .

Karaboudjan

 KARABOUDJAN . . . that's an Armenian name. Karaboudjan . . .

 An Armenian name. So . . . now what? . . . That doesn't help me much!

 HELP! HELP!

 What's going on? . . .

 That was my landlady's voice. I must go and see what's happened.

It was a Japanese or a Chinese gentleman with a letter for you, Mr Tintin. But just as he was going to give it to me a car came by, and stopped . . .

. . . outside the door. Three men got out; they attacked the Chinese gentleman and knocked him down! . . . Of course I shouted: 'Help! Help!' but one of the gangsters threatened me with a huge revolver, as big as that! Then they threw the Japanese gentleman into their car and drove off . . . with the letter addressed to you . . .

A tin + a drowned man + five counterfeit coins + Karaboudjan + a Japanese + a letter + a kidnapping = a real Chinese puzzle.

 The next morning . . .

 RRRING RRRING RRRING

 Hello? . . . Yes . . . Oh, it's you! . . . What's the news? . . . What? . . .

Yes, the drowned man has been identified: the one who had the mysterious bit of paper and the five dud coins. His name was Herbert Dawes: he was a sailor from the merchant-ship KARABOUDJAN.

The merchant-ship KARABOUDJAN! Did you say KARABOUDJAN? . . .

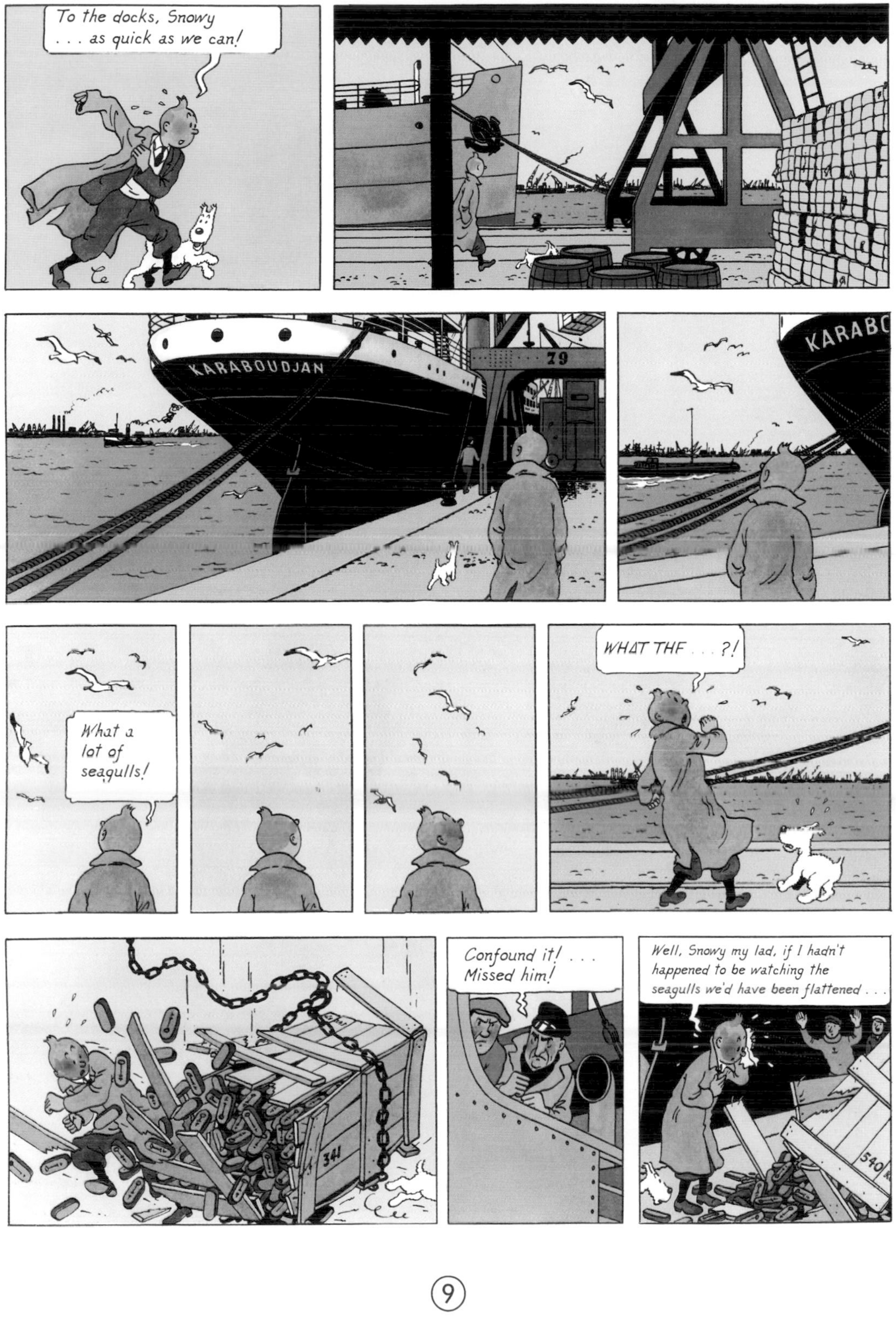
To the docks, Snowy . . . as quick as we can!
KARABOUDJAN
79
KARABO
What a lot of seagulls!
WHAT THE . . . ?!
341
Confound it! . . . Missed him!
Well, Snowy my lad, if I hadn't happened to be watching the seagulls we'd have been flattened . . .
540

 What happened? . . .

Oh, it's you! Well, I just missed being squashed by that heavy crate! . . . But what are you doing here?

The chain broke . . .

 We are going aboard the KARABOUDJAN to inquire about the sailor who was drowned.

Are you? May I come too? It would give me a chance to look round the ship . . .

 Will you be long on board?

No, only about half an hour.

 He's coming aboard with the two detectives!

You take care of him, while I talk to them . . . He mustn't go back on shore!

I get it!

 All right then? . . . I'll wait for you here in half an hour . . .

Here? . . . Good.

 How do you do, Mister Mate. We've come about that unfortunate sailor . . .

I'm at your service, gentlemen. Will you come into my cabin? We can talk more easily there . . .

 Mind the step . . .

Yes, I see it.

 . . . and the door is a bit low . . .

. . . so this sailor used to drink. On the night of his death you met him in the town, very drunk; then he fell into the water trying to get back to the ship. Plain as a pikestaff!

To be precise: plain as a pikestaff.

Excuse me, Mister Mate. I just wanted to tell you I've finished that job.

Good, I'll come and see.

As a matter of fact, we must go too. We have already taken up too much of your time.

Not at all! I'm delighted to have been able to help.

Yes, that door really is a little low . . .

A little low, yes . . .

A little too low . . .

The young man who came aboard with you asked me to say that he couldn't wait: he's just gone.

Oh! Tintin! . . . We'd quite forgotten him . . .

Mind the step.

Goodbye!

Goodbye!

What can have happened to Tintin?

They've put me in the bottom of the hold, the brutes! I wonder . . . Ah! someone's coming.

Are you keeping up this little joke for long?

Yes and no, my young friend. It all depends . . .

At least tell me why I'm tied up here in the hold . . .

It's no use pretending. You know why better than we do.

But . . .

SLAM

Snowy!! Good old Snowy! How did you get in here? . . . It must have been while those two scoundrels . . .

Ssh! . . . Listen . . .

TOOOOOT

We're sailing . . . for an unknown destination. But it's no good rotting away down here. Snowy, bite through these ropes and we'll take the first chance we get to say goodbye to these pirates!

Here's a coded radio message just in from the Boss. Read it . . .

'Send T to the bottom'

And I've just sent Pedro down with some food for him! . . . Oh well! I'll take a rope and a lump of lead, and that'll soon fix him.

It's very kind of you to bring me that, but how am I going to eat with my hands tied behind my back?

You're right, I'll have to loosen them a bit. But mind you, no tricks . . .

. . . make one false move . . . you get me? . . .

?

. . . he asked me to free his hands so he could eat; but as soon as I bent down he hit me a terrific crack . . .

. . . and that's nothing to what the mate will do to you!

12

Idiot! . . . Nitwit! . . . Now we'll have to find him, you fool!

. . . and now he's got a gun.

I hope these are cases of food. Then we can withstand a siege behind our barricade! Anyway . . .

Let's see . . .

Great snakes! . . . Tins of crab!

No doubt about it, these are the same as the tin we tried to find! . . .

We'll sort that out later. Let's go on checking our stores.

Champagne too! Snowy my boy, our supplies are taken care of!

And how!

Let me offer you a drink, Snowy . . .

Ssh! . . .

Quiet! . . . They're looking for us! They mustn't find us . . .

BANG

It's no good trying to open that door. He'll have barricaded himself in. We'll starve him out: he's nothing to eat . . .

. . . that's what you think, gentlemen!

!?

Opium! . . .

So we've managed to get ourselves mixed up with drug-runners!

This certainly changes everything! They were quite right: we've nothing to eat! . . .

Who cares? We've plenty to drink!

Let's see if we can't get out somehow.

Golly, how she rolls!

No, we can't reach the port-hole above; it's too far . . .

Unless . . . yes, I've got an idea . . .

Meanwhile . . .

Mister Mate, the Captain wants you . . .

The Captain? . . . What does he want, the old drunkard?

Yes, I sent f-f-for you, Mister Mate; it's wicked! I'm . . . it's wicked! . . . I'm being allowed to d-die of thirst! . . . I . . . I haven't a d-d-drop of whisky!

That's quite intolerable, Captain. I'll have some sent in at once.

At any rate, you-you-you are my friend, Mr Allan. You're the only one who . . . one who . . . who . . .

Of course, of course, you know I wouldn't deprive you of whisky for anything in the world . . .

For then I'll be the boss on this ship and do just as I like!

That night . . .

Now it's dark I'll try out my plan.

BONK

?

Let's have another shot.

No one there! But what . . . ?

. . . perhaps it's the whisky . . .

Ssh! . . . Not a sound!

Who-who . . . who are you?

Someone forced to sail in this vile tub and . . .

Vile tub? . . . I . . . d-d-do you know I'm Captain Haddock! And I can have you -y-y-you clapped in irons!

Thanks! I've just got out of them! I've spent enough time in your hold with its cargo of opium!

O-o-opium? There's opium in the hold? . . . In my hold . . . m-m-mine? . . .

Didn't you know?

Opium! . . . But h-h-how? . . . It's frightful! . . . I'm an hon . . . an honest man . . . and not . . . but who . . . ? It must be Allan, the f-first mate, who has . . . he . . . he's double-crossing me . . .

Listen, you must help me. And you must promise to stop drinking. Think of your reputation, Captain! What would your old mother say if she saw you in such a state? . . .

M-m-my old mother? . . .

There, there, Captain! . . .

Boo hoo . . . Boo . . . hoo . . . hoo Booh . . . hoo *Booh . . . hoo.*

For goodness' sake be quiet . . .

Boo . . . hoo . . . Mummy! M-M-Mummy!

Let's go and see. Perhaps he's gone crazy . . .

Too late! I'm trapped . . .

Mummy . . . Boo . . . hoo . . . hoo . . .

What's going on here? . . .

Mummy . . . Boo . . . hoo . . . hoo . . .

I'm a miserable wretch . . .

Here, drink this . . . You'll feel better . . .

FFFFH

N-n-no . . . I . . . I promised him not to drink . . . and I won't any more!

Who did you promise that to? . . .

To the y-y-young man who . . . who who . . . who was here . . .

What young man? Answer me!

By thunder!

I don't know . . . I've never seen him before.

The little devil! So he managed to get in here! . . . Luckily that drunken bawling scared him off. But he may try to come back . . .

Jumbo, stay and watch this port-hole. If anyone tries to climb in here, get him. Understand? . . . here's a gun . . .

Right.

We must settle his hash! We'll blow in the door of the hold where he's hiding!

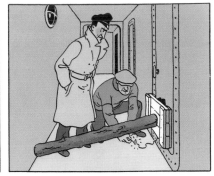

That's it! . . . Take cover . . .

BOOM

That must have knocked him out . . .

Or else he's shamming . . .

The swine!

BANG

BANG
BANG
BANG

A champagne cork!

In that case . . .

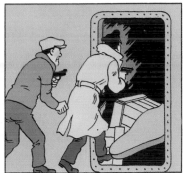

BANG

?

Quick! Back again! . . .

?!? ++! *?

I watched the port-hole carefully, Mister Mate, but not the locker under the bunk . . . And that's where he was hiding! . . .

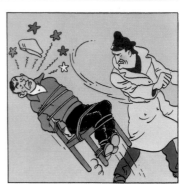

!!

Mister Mate, the wireless operator! . . . I just found him, bound and gagged!

It's a rum thing, Mister Mate! . . . The longboat has vanished!

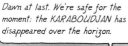

Dawn at last. We're safe for the moment: the KARABOUDJAN has disappeared over the horizon.

But we're not out of trouble yet! We must be sixty miles from the Spanish coast. We must save our energy. You sleep for a bit. Then I'll have a rest while you take a turn at the oars.

OK.

BANG

Heavens, I'm thirsty! ... And cold! ...

I remember: there's a keg of fresh water here, and biscuits ...

... and some rum!

But I swore never to drink again, and I'll keep my word!

Maybe if I only had a little drop ...

... just to warm myself up?

Aaaah! ... That's the stuff to keep the cold out!

Now, just one more sip ...

and I'll throw it away ...

Hello, it's empty already!

Poor l-l-little chap! He's fast asleep!

But he must be f-f-frightfully c-c-cold, too ...

Aha! I've got an idea

!?

Our oars! Hey! . . .
You're burning our oars!
Have you gone mad? . . .

Ah! here's
a bucket!

If . . . if you p-p-put that out . . .
y-you'll have to settle with m-m-me,
you miserable whipper-snapper . . .

Let go of that bucket, you
meddlesome cabin-boy!

?

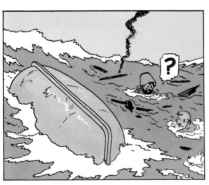

?

What have I done? Oh, Columbus
. . . What have I done!

You've got us into a fine
mess . . .

I'm sorry . . . I'm sorry! . . . I'm a
miserable wretch . . . I drank the
rum from the locker . . . I'm
sorry! . . .

Ssh! . . .

A seaplane! . . .
We're saved! . . .

It's got Moroccan
markings: CN.

RAT
TAT   TAT
TAT
TAT   TAT
TAT
TAT

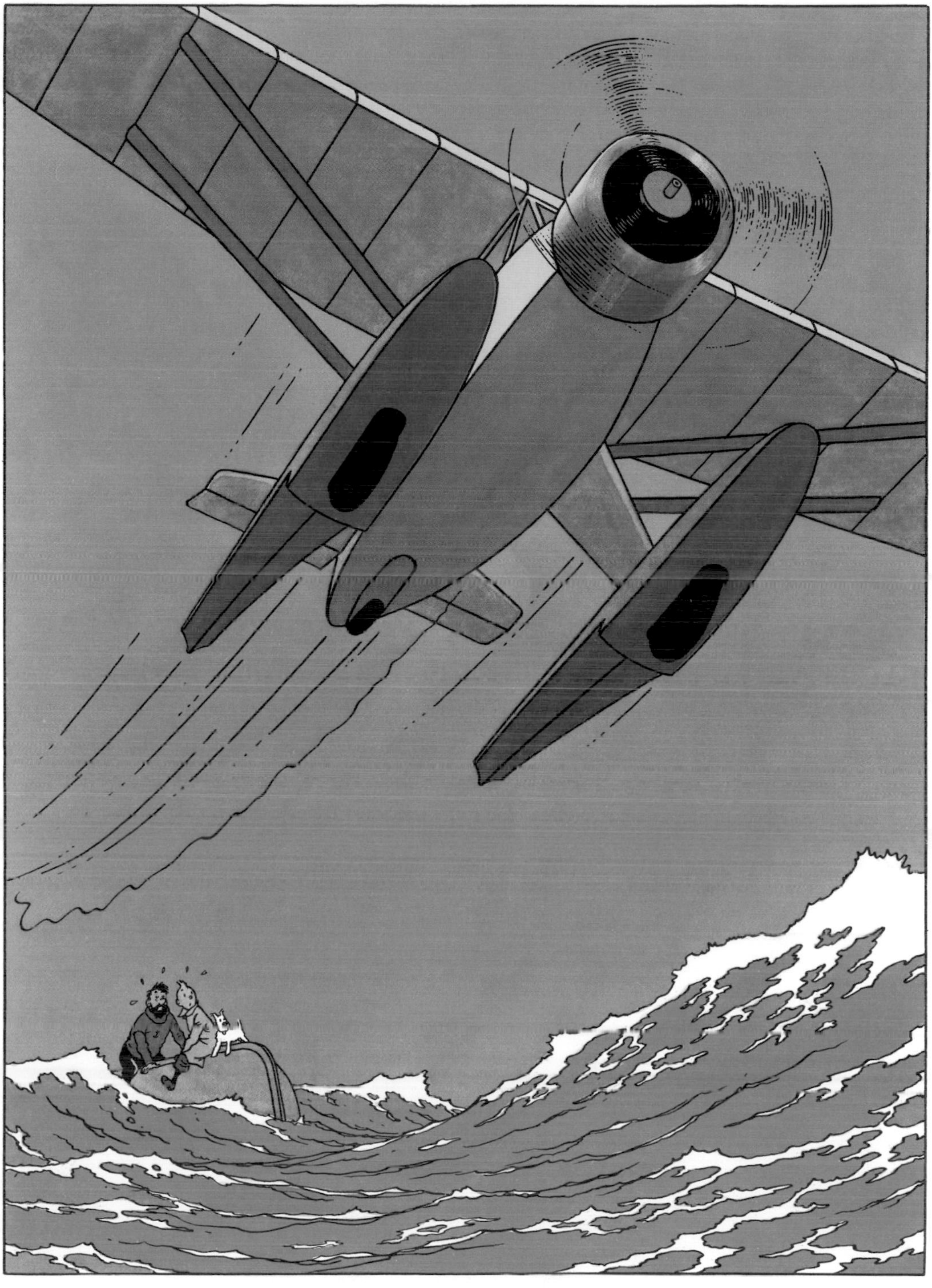

Just our luck! . . . A single bullet, and it has to go and cut the main ignition lead! But it won't take long to mend.

You do it. I'll keep an eye on them . . .

Look, they're both on the same side. I'll dive: swim underwater as far as I can, beyond them, and when I come up I should be out of their sight, and near the plane.

You can't possibly . . .

Getting on?

Yes, it's nearly done.

Finished?

That's it! . . . I'll just fix the last bolt.

Hands up!

Get back . . . and no tricks! I'm a good shot!

He's done it! . . . What a boy! . . .

Good. Try and find some rope to tie up these two toughs.

Tie them up? Why? . . . Let's just pitch them into the sea! They didn't worry about shooting us up, the gangsters!

I know, but we aren't gangsters! . . . Come on, Captain, tie them up and let's get going.

Now then: who hired you two for this shady business?

So! I see why you pretended to be so big-hearted! You wanted to pump us! Well, we aren't talking! . . .

As you like. But perhaps you'll find your tongues when the police get their hands on you.

Hey, can you fly an aeroplane? . . .

You're sure this is the right direction for Spain? . . .

Er . . . yes . . . but it remains to be seen if we'll get there. We're in for a rough time.

Oh, Columbus, this is frightful! . . . We'll never come through alive!

Oho, a bottle! . . . Now if only it were whisky . . .

And it is whisky! . . .

Since we've got to die, I may as well have one last bottle . . .

Hey, it looks f-f-fun doing that . . . L-l-let me have a go!

This is hardly the moment . . .

B-b-but I w-w-want to! . . .

Leave that alone! . . .

Whew, what luck! . . . I just managed to right her . . .

Quick, look behind you!

No good, he can't hear above the engine.

N-n-now then you whippersnapper! I don't c-c-care for your tricks! . . .

W-w-will y-you let me t-take over: yes or no? . . . One . . . two . . . three . . .

Leave me alone!

Then take that, you pig-headed . . .

Great snakes!
What happened?

Help! . . . We're going
to crash . . .

That was a near thing!

Good heavens! . . . The two
prisoners? . . . They're still
in the plane . . .

A camel! . . .

A camel? . . . But there aren't any camels in Spain . . .

Unfortunately we aren't in Spain! . . . We're in the middle of the Sahara Desert!

In the middle of the Sahara! . . . then that animal . . . that animal . . . that animal died of . . . died of . . .

. . . died of thirst, of course!

What's the matter? . . . Feeling faint?

The land of thirst! . . . The land of thirst! . . .

The land of thirst . . .

Courage, Captain, courage! We aren't finished yet.

It looks as if he's at the end of his tether.

The land of thirst . . .

The prisoners have gone!

I see! Their ropes were almost burnt through: it didn't take much to break them.

The land of thirst . . .

Look over there . . . they're too far away now for us to catch them up. Never mind . . .

Come on, Captain! Perhaps we shall be lucky and come across a well!

The land of thirst . . .

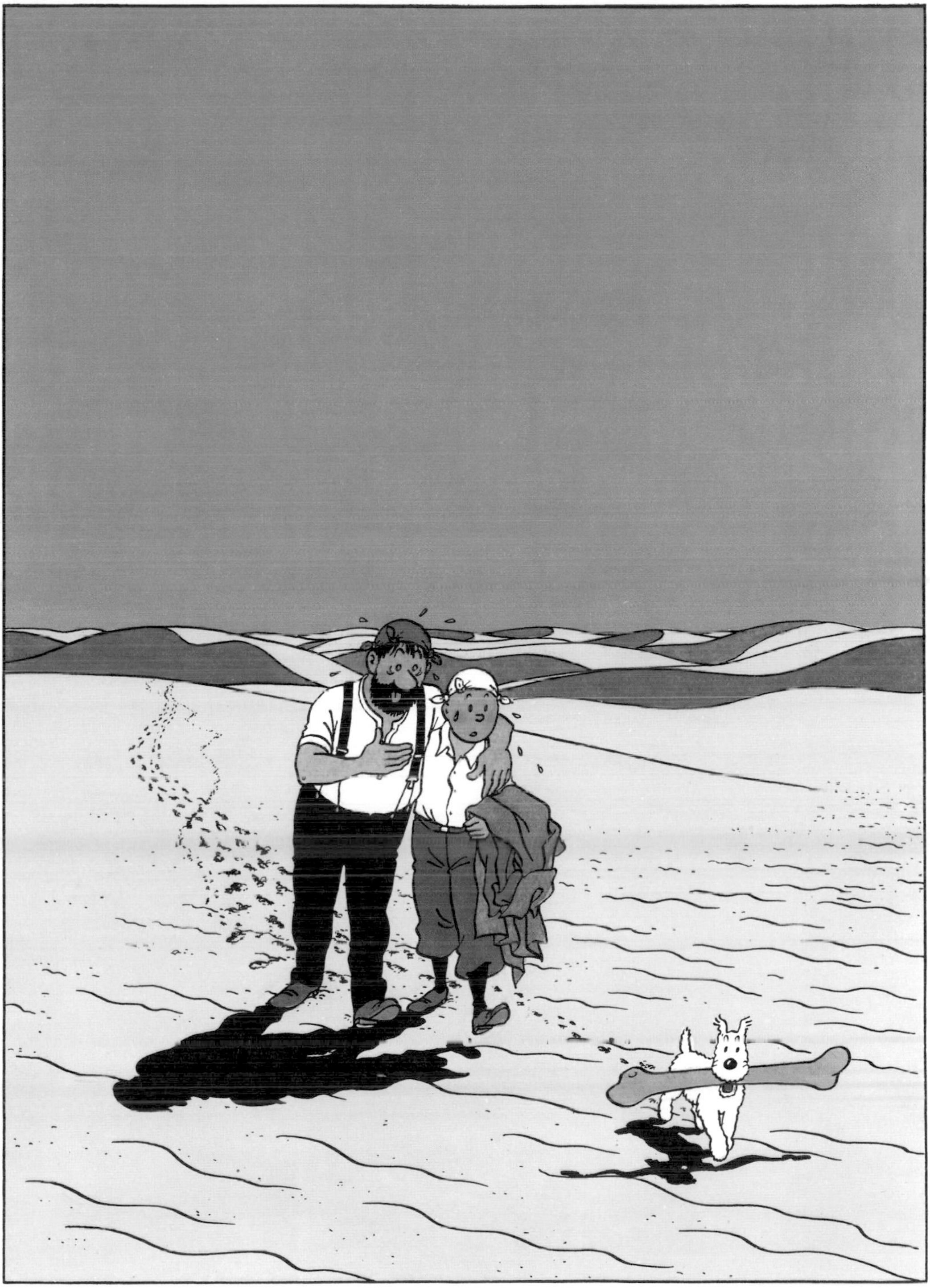

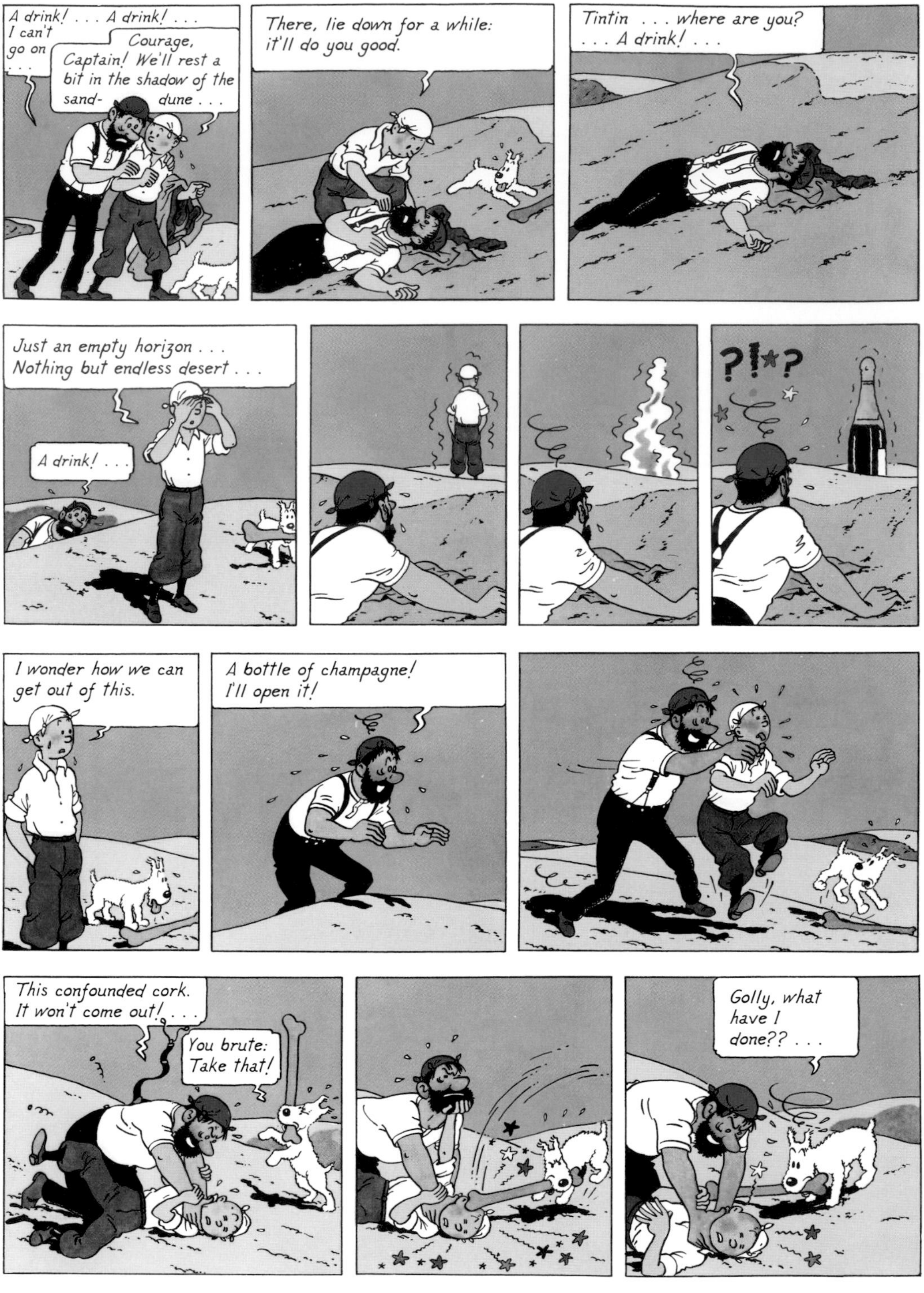
A drink! . . . A drink! . . . I can't go on . . .
Courage, Captain! We'll rest a bit in the shadow of the sand-dune . . .
There, lie down for a while: it'll do you good.
Tintin . . . where are you? . . . A drink! . . .
Just an empty horizon . . . Nothing but endless desert . . .
A drink! . . .
?!*?
I wonder how we can get out of this.
A bottle of champagne! I'll open it!
This confounded cork. It won't come out! . . .
You brute: Take that!
Golly, what have I done?? . . .

Didn't I tell you it was a mirage? There isn't a lake.

But I saw it . . .

Some hours later . . .

سدل سع ب ط تن ه ها د لا ى...

و ع س؟

م ه ل ا لس ت!

Aha! . . . There's a bottle of wine!

Where can he see a bottle?

I'll uncork it . . .

??!

BOURG
VIED

I hear you call help?

?!?!

Whew! What a ghastly nightmare!

Where am I? . . . What happened? . . .

You come with me to Lieutenant.

He come, sir . . . the young boy.

Ah! there you are. Come in! I'm glad to see you on your feet again.

I'm Lieutenant Delcourt, in command of the outpost of Afghar.

How do you do, Lieutenant. My name is Tintin. But how . . .

. . . how did you get here? . . . At about midday yesterday my men noticed a column of smoke on the southern horizon. I immediately thought it might be an aeroplane and sent out a patrol. They saw your tracks, found you unconscious, and brought you in.

Oh! Did they find my friend too? . . .

Here he is! . . . Come in, come in. Ahmed, bring three glasses and some drinks . . .

So the smoke was from a plane, then?

Yes, we came down with quite a bump. The machine turned over and caught fire . . .

No thank you. I never drink spirits.

No? . . . Really?

?

Er . . . er . . . no thank you, Lieutenant. I . . . don't either. I . . . I never touch spirits . . .

You don't either? . . . Well, I won't press you.

Anyway, you saved our lives all right, Lieutenant. Without you and your camel patrol we should have died of thirst.

That's why you ought to have a drink with me! . . . But never mind about that. I'd rather you told me what brings you to this forsaken land.

. . . and here is the latest news. Yesterday's severe gales caused a number of losses to shipping. The steamship TANGANYIKA sank near Vigo, but her crew were all taken off. The merchant vessel JUPITER has been driven ashore, but her crew are safe. An SOS was also picked up from the merchant-ship . . .

. . . KARABOUDJAN. Another vessel, the BENARES, went at once to the aid of the KARABOUDJAN and searched all night near the position given in the distress signal. No wreckage and no survivors were found. It must therefore be presumed that the KARABOUDJAN went down with all hands . . . !

That's odd, don't you think?

I should say so! The KARABOUDJAN isn't a cockleshell, to sink without time to launch the boats. It's unbelievable!

That's what I think . . . Lieutenant, is there any way we could leave today? I'm anxious to get to the coast as soon as possible. I'll tell you why.

So soon?. . . Yes, it can be done. It should be enough if I send two guides with you. That area has been quite safe for a   couple of months now.

Two hours later . . .

Allah protect them!

Next morning . . .

A wireless message has just come in, sir . . .

Thank you.

MOST URGENT
T.O.1026 S.C.
Twenty Arab riders reported near Timmin proceeding to Wells of Kefheir. Stop. Dispatch patrol.

By Jupiter! . . . The Wells of Kefheir lie on the route Tintin and his friend are taking! . . .

Ahmed, send my section leaders here at once. And by the way, what did you do with the bottles which were here yesterday?

I not know, sir. I not touch bottles, sir.

Now I'll just have a good swig of this: nobody's watching me.

See! . . . Kefheir . . .

Your very good health, my friends!

CRACK

BANG
BANG
BANG

The Berbers!

Quick! Behind the sanddune! . . . Dismount!

And the Lieutenant said this was a safe area!

Yah! The scoundrels!

They'll pay for this! . . .

Now, let them come: I'm ready for them!

Crumbs! One of them has picked me for a target.

Aha! I've spotted him . . . Just you wait, my friend: I'll show you a thing or two!

By the beard of the Prophet! . . . I will get you this time! . . .

BANG

BANG

Not bad shooting, eh? . . .

BANG   BANG

So! I've managed to crawl behind them without being seen . . .

BANG

Now for the boy: he is the best shot . . .

BANG

BANG

BANG

WHIZZZ

CRACK

!

BANG

?

BANG

BANG

BANG

ZZZZ

REVENGE!

BANG

REVENGE!

REVENGE!

REVENGE!

BANG

BANG

Swine! . . . Jellyfish! . . . Tramps! . . . Troglodytes! . . . Toffee-noses! . . .

?

Captain! Stop, Captain! . . . You'll get yourself killed! . . .

Savages! . . . Aztecs! . . . Toads! . . . Carpet-sellers! . . . Iconoclasts! . . .

Some saint must watch over drunkards! . . . It's a miracle he hasn't been hit . . .

Rats! . . . Ectoplasms! . . . Freshwater swabs! . . . Cannibals! . . . Bashi-bazouks! . . . Caterpillars! . . .

Cowards! . . . Baboons! . . . Parasites! . . . Pockmarks! . . .

Great snakes! . . . He's got them on the run! . . .

. . . and if you come back you'll feel my rifle-butt! . . .

Well done, Captain! . . . Wonderful! . . .

If those savages had just waited, I'd have shown them! . . . But they ran like rabbits . . . except one who sneaked up on me from behind, the pirate . . .

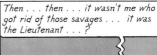

Charge! . . . After them! . . . Take them prisoner! . . .

It's the Lieutenant! . . .

Then . . . then . . . it wasn't me who got rid of those savages . . . it was the Lieutenant . . . ?

We turned up at the right moment, didn't we? . . .

In the nick of time, Lieutenant. But what made you come here?

That's soon explained. This morning I received a radio warning of raiders near Kefheir. We jumped into the saddle right away . . . and here we are! . . .

And now, as soon as my men return with their prisoners we'll all ride north together, to prevent further incidents like this.

After several days' journey, Tintin and the Captain come to Bagghar, a large Moroccan port . . .

First we'll go to the harbour-master. Perhaps he can give us news of the KARABOUDJAN.

Good idea . . .

!

?

Tintin! . . . Tintin! . . . Where are you going?

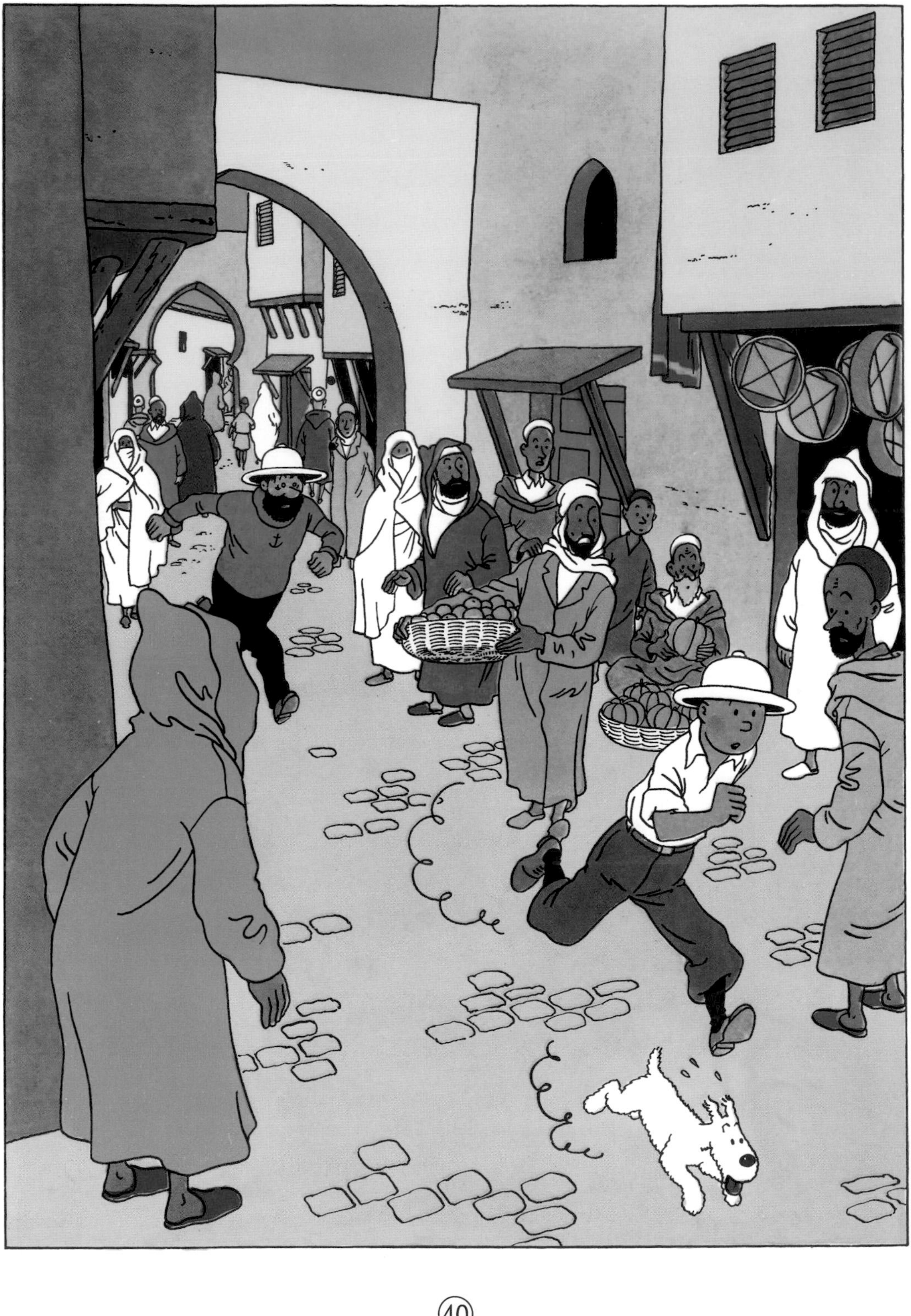

Out of my way, you!

Move along there! Move along!

Bunch of savages! Now I've lost Tintin. What's got into him, I wonder?

Careful! . . . I mustn't lose sight of him.

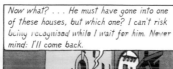
Now what? . . . He must have gone into one of these houses, but which one? I can't risk being recognised while I wait for him. Never mind: I'll come back.

How shall I ever find Tintin?

The first thing is to find the Captain. I hope he's had the sense to go straight to the harbour-master's office and wait for me there.

And now—now for the h-h-harbour-master! ... H-h-how much, boy?

Five francs.

P-P-POLICE! PO-PO-POLICE!

What's up this time?

I ... I ... it's disgraceful! ... My wallet's been stolen! ... I'll s-s-sue th-them! ... R-r-robbers! ... M-m-my wallet! ...

It's dis-gr-graceful! ... A city of p-p-pick-p-p-pockets ... I w-w-want my wallet! ...

Here's your wallet! ... Stop all that row! ... It had fallen out of your pocket. And don't rouse the whole neighbourhood another time!

Now go home! ... If you make any more trouble, we'll run you in. Understand?

OK, a-a-admiral!

Yo-ho ♩ ♩ and ♪up ♪ she ♩ rises ♫

DJEBEL AMILAH

B-b-blistering barnacles! ... that's the K-K-KARABOUDJAN! Police! ... Arrest them! ... Police! ... P-p-police!

P-P-POLICE! PO-POLICE!

I t-t-tell you it's the KARABOUD-BOUD-BOUDJAN, Blistering barnacles! I am ... I am her Captain! ... It's not the DJEBEL-what's it ... You must arrest the l-l-lot of them!

Come along! That's enough!

But I tell you that is the K-K-KARABOUDJAN! ... and she's full of op-opium!

This wretched door won't open! . . .

The noise of an engine! . . . They must have a car!

Too late!

Another car! . . . I'll grab it: I must save the Captain at all costs!

That's got her started! . . . Off we go, full speed ahead! . . .

What's up? Why are we going backwards? . . .

PAAARP! PAAARP! PAAARP!

Stop! The car's horn must have got stuck.

I mustn't let them get away!

Saved! . . . There's a taxi!

Taxi! To the Central Station!

Quick, follow that car!

?   ?

Be so good as to get out, young man: I was first.

I beg your pardon, sir, but I was before you!

My dear sir, I am not in the habit of arguing with puppies. Get out! At once! . . . I have to be at the Central Station in fifteen minutes.

And I must get to the hospital urgently . . .

as I've just been bitten by this mad dog!

Quick, driver, follow that car!

Which car, sir?

Which car? . . . Why that one . . . Heavens! It's gone!

Now all I can do is find the alley where I lost the mate of the KARABOUDJAN.

But I ought to wear a burnous to go there, otherwise I might be recognised.

Ah! here's an old clothes shop . . . but . . . but surely . . . I can't be mistaken.

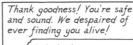

My old friends Thomson and Thompson.

Thank goodness! You're safe and sound. We despaired of ever finding you alive!

I think it's extraordinary, he recognised us at once, in spite of our disguise!

Now tell us: what happened on the KARABOUDJAN? We were amazed when they handed us your wireless signal: 'Have been imprisoned aboard KARABOUDJAN. Am leaving vessel. Cargo includes opium. TINTIN.' We took the first plane for Bagghar . . .

. . . the KARABOUDJAN's next port of call. Then we heard about the shipwreck. Are you certain she was carrying opium?

Quite certain: the drug was hidden in tins bearing a label with a red crab on it, and the words 'EXTRA FINE CRAB'.

Tins of crab? . . . That reminds me . . .

I saw one in the shop where we bought our burnouses just now.

Did you? Quick let's go and see.

It's gone!

What have you done with the tin of crab that was on the table?

It's here, sidi. I put tin here in the cupboard.

That's the one! I recognise the label: it's the same.

Open that tin!

There, sidi . . .

Look!

It's crab!

Of course, sidi, there is crab. Good crab, sidi, best quality . . .

Yes, it's crab all right . . . And yet I saw the same tins aboard the KARABOUDJAN, and they contained opium.

Hmm! . . . Very odd.

To be precise: very odd; in fact, very queer . . .

Tell me: where did you buy this tin?

From Mohammed Ben Ali, sidi; the shop on the corner . . .

46

Now for Mohammed Ben Ali.

Look!

Hmm, no one about?

These are the same tins, all right.

To be precise: no one about...

Hi! Anybody there!

Hi! Anybody there?

? ?

CRASH

BANG

Good gracious! Something's happened to him...

Thomson!... Thomson! ...Where are you?

BANG

CRASH

?

?? ?

!

All right?

Look out, there's a step.

Nothing broken?

No, all's well.

Yes, all's well.

Mind your hat!...

What are you doing here?

Oh! Are you the owner of this shop?

I would like the name and address of the supplier who sold you the tins of crab you have in your shop.

The tins of crab? They came from Omar Ben Salaad, sidi, the biggest trader in Bagghar. He is very rich, sidi, very very rich . . . He has a magnificent palace, with many horses and cars; he has great estates in the south; he even has a flying machine, sidi, which some people call an aeroplane . . .

Indeed! . . . Thank you very much.

Will you help me, and make discreet inquiries about this Omar Ben Salaad? . . . Among other things, try and find out the registration number of his private plane. But you must be discreet, very discreet.

My friend, you can count on us. We are the soul of discretion. 'Mum's the word', that's our motto.

Yes, that's our motto: 'Dumb's the word' . . .

Now to rescue the Captain. First I must get the right clothes . . .

Hello Mister Mate? . . . This is Tom . . . Yes, we got the Captain. He made a bit of a row but the wharves were deserted and no one heard us . . . What? You'll be along in an hour? . . . OK.

Meanwhile . . .

RUE DE L'OUE

Does Mr Omar Ben Salaad live here? . . . We'd like a word with him.

My master has just gone out, sidi. See, there he is on his donkey . . .

So that's him.

Make way! Make way for the mighty Omar Ben Salaad!

Let's follow him.

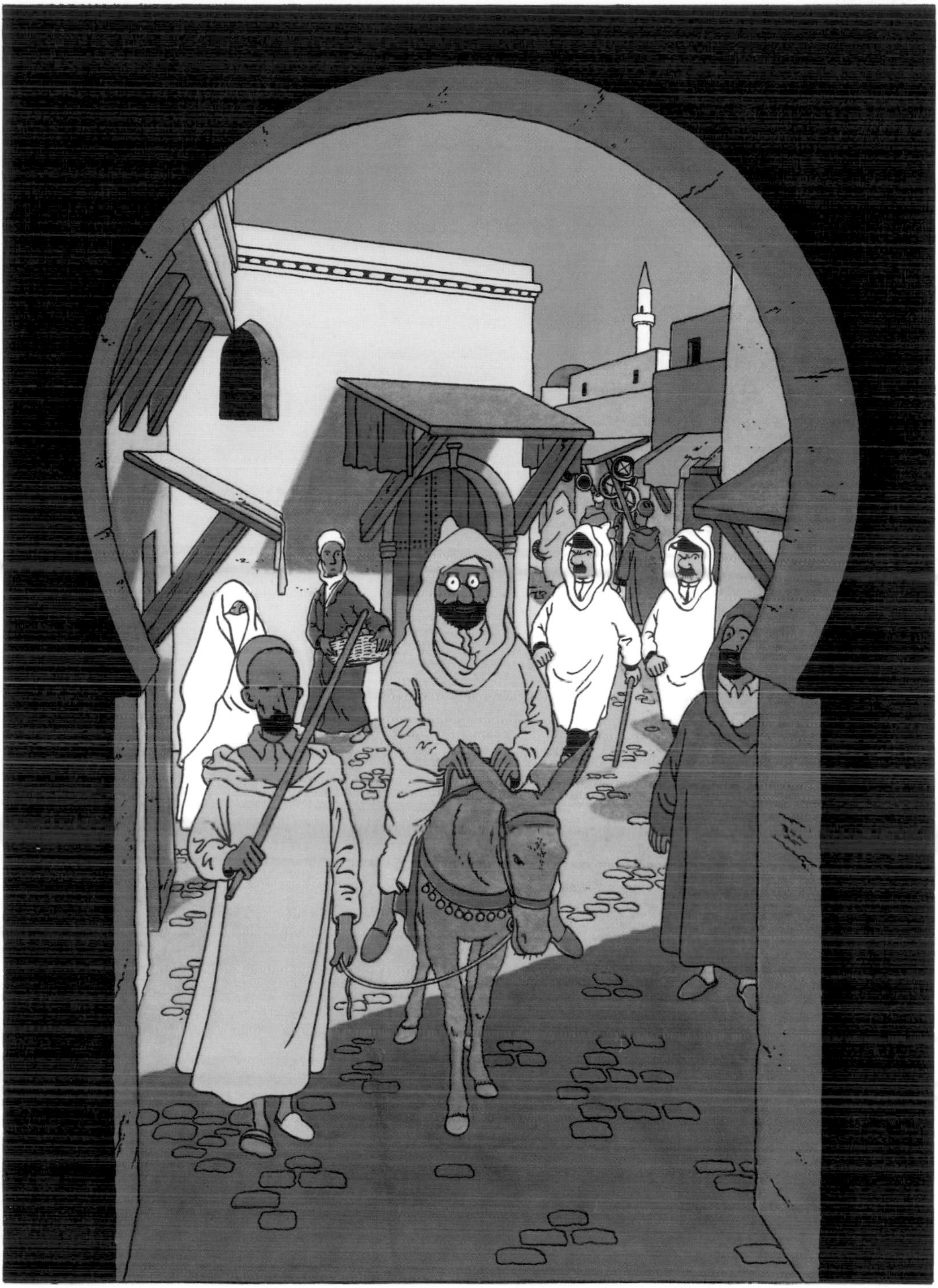

He's gone in there. Shall we follow?

Of course we follow . . .

VISITORS TO THE MOSQUE ARE ASKED TO REMOVE THEIR SHOES

? ?

One hour later . . .

How did that happen? . . .

These confounded paving stones! I tripped over.

Whew! . . . What a narrow escape!

I must risk everything and follow him. If I'm questioned, I've come to beg alms!

50

What do you want here? ...

Alms, for the love of Allah, the Prophet will reward you ...

Out you go, verminous beggar! Crawling worm! Begone, son of a mangy dog!

How very polite! ...

Whew! ... This is going to be harder than I thought. What next? But where's Snowy, I wonder?

By the beard of the Prophet! ... Thief!

?!

Come back, you robber! Give me my joint!

Now or never! ...

A whole joint! ... Vile dog! If ever I see it again ... !

Tell me, is Sidi Allan here? ...

Crumbs! He's back already!

Yes, Abd El Drachm, he has just come.

Quick! ... I must hide in the cellar.

Good, I'll go to him. Farewell.

Heavens! He's coming down here!

Where's he gone! . . . He can't have vanished into thin air! . . .

No secret passage, and no trap-door; the walls and floor sound absolutely solid. It must be magic.

WOOAH!

Snowy! . . . You frightened the life out of me!

You rascal, now I see. You hid in the ventilator shaft to eat that joint!

As for me, Snowy, I'm like old Diogenes, seeking a man! You've never heard of Diogenes! . . . He was a philosopher in ancient Greece, and he lived in a barrel . . .

Lived in a barrel! . . . In a barrel, Snowy! . . . Great snakes! I think I've got it!

Let's see if this barrel will open . . .

And it does! There are hinges here!

Look Snowy . . . A way out!

And a door the other end! We're certainly on the right track, Snowy . . .

Hooray! The tins of crab from the KARABOUDJAN.

BANDITS!

BRUTES!

That's the Captain's voice!...

Yell as loud as you like; no one can hear you. Why not be sensible? Now for the last time: where is Tintin?

HERE!...

?

Hands up!... No one move! You there, untie the Captain...

Give me your hand, Tintin!... Give me your hand!...

My automatic!

Too late!

This way! Quick! . . .

BANG

What have I done? . . . Oh Columbus! . . . What . . .

It's no good moaning: what's done is done. The thing now is to get away . . .

In here . . . they're shooting at us.

Trapped!

We've got them! This is the only exit!

Hooray! . . . That's got them beating a retreat! . . .

BANG BANG BANG

Ooooh! All that wine! . . . What a terrible waste! . . .

Now then, no nonsense! . . . This isn't the time for drinking!

What do you take me for? A drunkard?

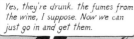

What's happening! . . . My head's reeling . . .

I'm the king of the castle

They're tight!

Ta - ra - ra - boom - de - ay

For tonight we'll merry merry be, for tonight we'll merry merry be . . .

Yes, they're drunk. the fumes from the wine, I suppose. Now we can just go in and get them.

Ta - ra - ra boom . . .

We'll take this one. You bring the other.

Tiddley - om - pom - pom . . .

I'm the king of the caaa- -aastle . . .

That's enough! let go of that bottle! . . .

You bully! My bottle! . . . Treason! . . . Revenge! . . . Twister! . . . . Heretic! . . . Slave-trader! . . . Technocrat!

Buccaneer! Vegetarian! Politician!

If he makes trouble I'll soon settle his hash!

55

Pirate! . . . Corsair!

Quiet, you drunken old fool! . . .

HARLEQUIN!

HYDROCARBON!

ABORIGINE!

POLYNESIAN! GYROSCOPE!

?!

Revenge!

Blackamoor! . . . Anthracite! . . . Coconut! . . . Fuzzy-wuzzy! . . . Cannibal! . . .

Go on! Seek! Seek! Bite him!

Athropithecus! . . . Blackbird! . . .

Tiddley - om - pom - pom

Meanwhile . . .

See, the great Omar Ben Salaad has returned from the mosque.

Shall we go and ask him a few questions?

Good idea!

Master, two strangers are here and would speak with you. They say they are making some inquiries.

Good. Show them in; I will see them.

Mr Omar, we have been asked to carry out an investigation . . .

A discreet investigation, of course . . .

Oh? . . . And what is the object of your investigation?

A young friend of ours, called Tintin, suspects that you are concerned in drug-running.

Are you, Mr Salaad?

?!

By the beard of the Prophet! . . . Who dares suspect Omar Ben Salaad? . . . Get out, infidel dogs! Get out, or I'll have you flogged to death!

?

Omar Ben Salaad an opium smuggler! Well, that beats everything! But ... what's going on now? ...

Swine! ... Vampire! ...

It's him again!

Hooray! The police! ...

Arrest that Negro! ... He's a gangster, p-p-pirate ... He ... he ... he beat me with a st-stick ...

It's not a stick you need, it's a wallop with my truncheon!

At last, the police! ... Gentlemen, this is the man we have brought to justice.

To be precise: ... this is the man!

Some of your men come with me: there are more of them in the cellar!

The mate has escaped: and he's the most dangerous of the lot ...

He must have gone out the other way! ... If some of your men take care of the gangsters still in the cellar, we'll go after the mate.

We'll go down to the harbour. He's a sailor, so he'll probably make for there ...

? *Police! Police!*

Someone's stolen one of the motorboats I look after! A man jumped aboard and he was gone in a flash!

There he is! It's him! Quick, another boat!

Hey, she won't go! The painter! . . . You've forgotten to slip the painter!

Of course, we've forgotten the painter!

Wait: I've got a knife. It's quicker!

All right?

That's it!

We're overhauling him! . . . Our boat is faster than his!

By thunder! They're after me!

Confound it! . . . The engine's stalled! . . . Crumbs! Where are Thomson and Thompson?

Something's fouled the propeller . . .

A fishing net! . . . Fine! Off we go again . . .

Devil take him: He's on my tail again! . . .

Take that! . . .

. . . and that! . . .

. . . and that! . . .

The boat's lurching wildly! . . . What a fight! . . . Ah! One of them's getting up . . . Who? . . .

It's Tintin! . . . He's got the best of it! . . . He's swinging round, and coming back! . . .

Quick! Give me that telescope!

?!

Hooray! He's got the mate!
... So that's the lot from the
KARABOUD-
JAN! ...

Steady on, Sergeant! ... None of that! ... Thanks to
Captain Haddock we've arrested the DJEBEL AMILAH,
which is none other than the camouflaged
KARABOUDJAN, and rounded up the crew ...

Quickly!

There's someone
waiting for you
up there.

Heartiest congratulations,
Mr Tintin!

?

Who
is this
chap?

Allow me to introduce myself:
Bunji Kuraki of the Yokohama
police force. The police have
just freed me from the hold of
the KARABOUDJAN where I
was imprisoned. I was kidnapped
just as I was bringing you a
letter . . .

Oh! So it was
you . . .

Yes, I wanted to warn you of the
risk you were running. I was on
the track of this powerful, well-
organised gang, which operates even
in the Far East. One night I met a
sailor called Herbert Dawes . . .

. . . who was one of
my crew . . .

. . . and later
was drowned
. . .

That's it. He was drunk, and boasted
that he could get me some opium. To
prove it he showed me an empty tin,
which, he said, had contained the drug.
I asked him to bring me a full tin the
next day. But next day he did not come
and I was
kidnapped

And they must have done
away with him: but why
was a bit of a label found
on him, with the word
KARABOUDJAN,
in pencil?

Well, I asked him the name
of his ship. He was so
drunk I couldn't hear what
he mumbled. So he wrote
it on a scrap of the label,
but then he put the paper
in his own pocket . . .

Some days later . . .

. . . and it is thanks to the young
reporter, Tintin, that the entire
organisation of the Crab with the
Golden Claws today   find
themselves behind   bars.

This is the Home
Service. You are about
to hear a talk given
by Mr Haddock,
himself a sea-captain,
on the subject of . . .

. . . drink,
the sailor's
worst enemy.

RRRING

Good-morning, Mr Tintin . . . Your letters . . . and a parcel . . .

What's in this parcel?

Why not open it?

I don't trust this! . . . It might be a bomb! Those gangsters are capable of anything . . .

So many from an admirers

Now, let's listen to the Captain . . .

. . . for the sailor's worst enemy is not the raging storm; it is not the foaming wave . . .

. . . which pounds upon the bridge sweeping all before it; it is not the treacherous reef lurking beneath the sea, ready to rend the keel asunder; the sailor's worst enemy is drink!

Phew! . . . How hot these studios are! . . .

GLUG GLUG GLUG . . . . . .
. . . . . . CRASH . . .
. . . . . . ZZING . . . .
. . . . . . BRR . . . .
. . . .

What's happening?

This is the Home Service. We must apologise to our listeners for this break in transmission, but Captain Haddock has been taken ill . . .

Hello, Broadcasting House? This is Tintin. Have you any news of Captain Haddock? I hope it's nothing serious . . .

No, nothing serious. The Captain is much better already . . . Yes . . . No . . . He was taken ill after drinking a glass of water . . .

THE END

HERGÉ

THE REAL-LIFE INSPIRATION
BEHIND
TINTIN'S ADVENTURES

Written by Stuart Tett
with the collaboration of Studio Moulinsart.

Discover something new and exciting

HERGÉ

In the army

In 1940, World War II was under way. Even though Hergé joined the Belgian Army, he continued sending drawings to *Le Petit Vingtième* magazine for the latest Tintin adventure, *Land of Black Gold*. In April 1940, Hergé was given three weeks of leave from the army because of ill health.

He wrote a letter (shown at right) to readers of *Le Petit Vingtième*, apologizing for the gaps in the story and promising that "earthquakes, floods, tornadoes and bombardment notwithstanding," the adventure would begin again soon. But because of the war, *Le Petit Vingtième* magazine and its parent newspaper, *Le Vingtième Siècle*, closed down. Hergé soon began work on another adventure, *The Crab with the Golden Claws*, which would be published in a magazine named *Le Soir Jeunesse*.

about Tintin and his creator Hergé!

TINTIN

© HERGÉ - ML 2011 © Nicolas Borel Architecte: Christian de Portzamparc

If you look at the photo above of the Hergé Museum, you can see that a huge picture of Tintin decorates the front entrance. It comes from *The Crab with the Golden Claws*. Can you find it in the story? You can read more about the Hergé Museum in the Young Readers Edition of *The Broken Ear.*

THE TRUE STORY
...behind *The Crab with the Golden Claws*

Once upon a time...

When Hergé began writing this story, he spent much of his time working from home. But in 1950, he set up Studios Hergé—a whole company of artists—and began working in an office again. He liked to decorate with scenery from Tintin's adventures, as you can see on the opposite page! The 1965 photo shows Hergé in the lobby of the fifth floor at 162 Avenue Louise, Brussels, Belgium.

On the case!

At the beginning of *The Crab with the Golden Claws*, Thomson and Thompson are lucky to get some help from their smart friend Tintin. The quick-witted reporter realizes that an odd-looking can of crab meat is a clue in the Thom(p)sons' police investigation. As he races off to find the can, the two half-baked police detectives are left behind. Tintin is always one step ahead!

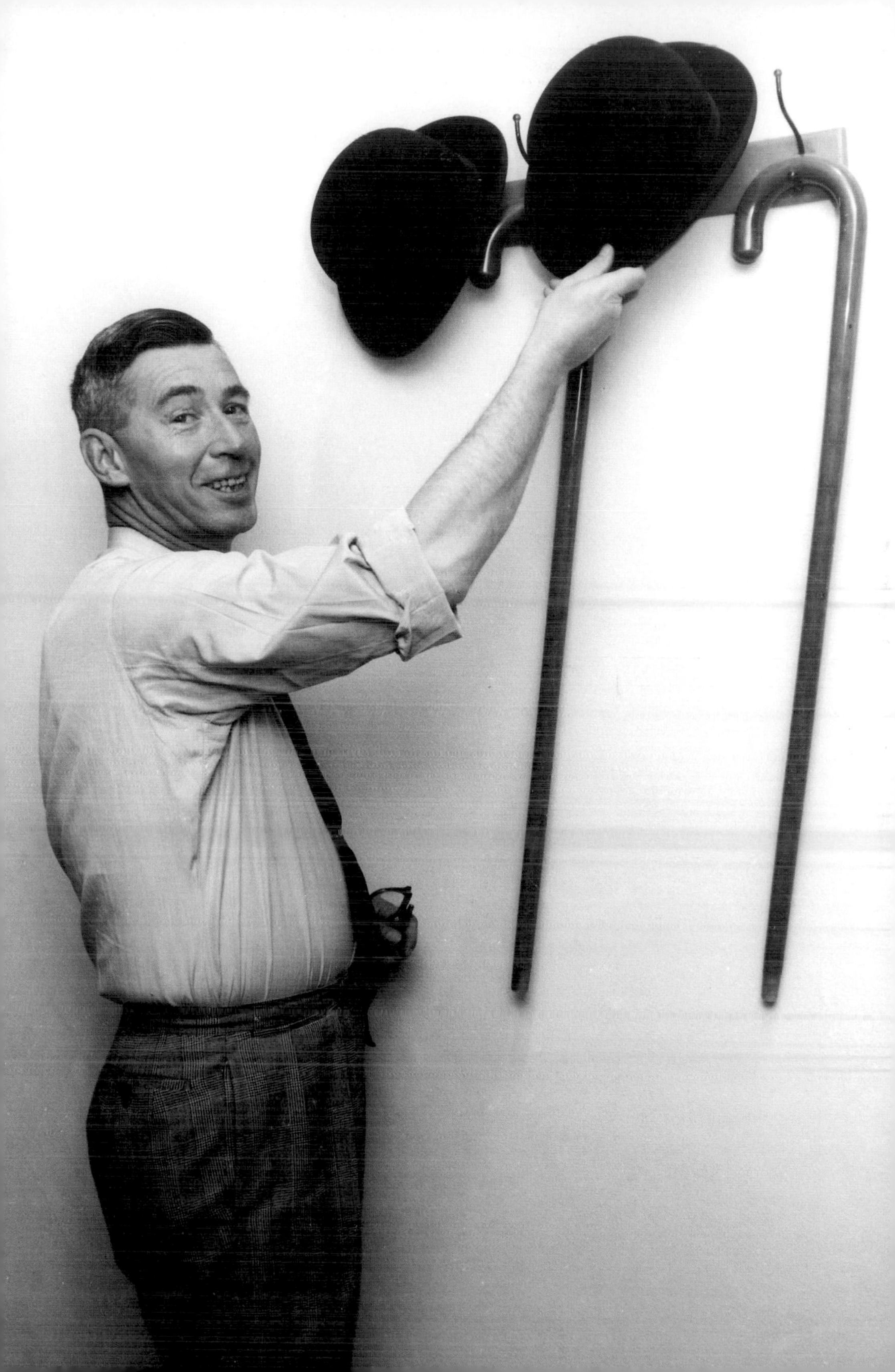

To the docks...

Although Tintin doesn't manage to find the can itself, he does discover the name of a ship—the *Karaboudjan*—written on a scrap of the label from the can. The clue takes Tintin to the docks to investigate.

Once upon a time…

Look at the photo below, taken from Hergé's archives. The *Karaboudjan* was copied from a real ship, the *Glengarry*. This 485-foot cargo vessel was first launched in 1920, but in November 1922, it ran aground while sailing on the Huangpu River (spelled Whangpoo at the time) in Shanghai. The ship survived a direct hit from a German bomber in 1940 while docked in London. The *Glengarry* was finally scrapped in 1952.

Escape the *Karaboudjan!*

Tintin and Captain Haddock manage to outwit the crooked crew of the *Karaboudjan*, which is led by first mate Allan. The heroes row away in a lifeboat. To make sure he drew it correctly, Hergé referred to a photo of a lifeboat from his archives. ▶

Once upon a time...

The photo shows a lifeboat carrying passengers from a French ocean liner called the *Georges-Philippar*. This ship sank in 1932 after a mysterious fire. One of the victims was the French reporter Albert Londres—one of the inspirations for Tintin—who was returning from an investigation in China.

Under attack!

Uh-oh! Everything was going so well until Captain Haddock started a fire in the lifeboat! When the boat capsizes, Tintin and the captain find themselves in the water. It looks like a plane is coming to rescue them, but they quickly realize it isn't friendly. Look above at the practice sketch Hergé drew of the plane swooping down to attack.

Once upon a time...

When he drew this airplane at the beginning of 1941, Hergé based it on a Bellanca 31-42 Senior Pacemaker. These airplanes were well-known for long-distance flights. Nevertheless, just like the forced landing Tintin and Haddock make in the Sahara Desert, there are true stories of the Bellanca Pacemaker falling short of its destination.

In June 1932, Polish aviator Stanislaus Hausner tried to complete a transatlantic flight from New York to Warsaw, Poland, in a Bellanca Pacemaker. He had to land in the middle of the sea and wasn't rescued until eight days later. In October 1936, Swedish pilot Kurt Björkwall attempted to fly across the Atlantic Ocean from New York to Stockholm, Sweden, but bad weather forced him to land 60 miles off the coast of Ireland! He was rescued by a French trawler ship.

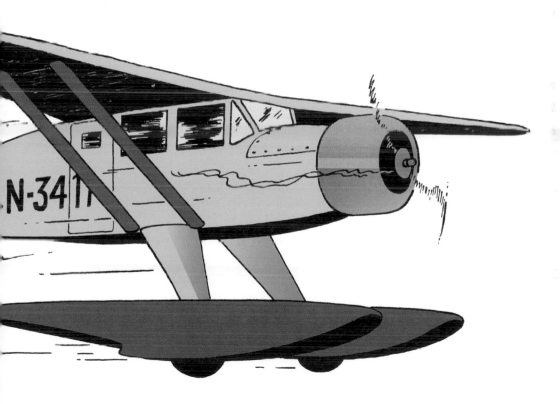

Crab, anyone?

Tintin and Captain Haddock had to escape from the *Karaboudjan* because they discovered the ship is being used for illegal smuggling. The villains hide their goods inside crab meat cans. Hergé designed his own can label, which looks so nice that today you can buy a coffee mug in Europe with the same design on it!

Once upon a time…

What were some of the first Tintin toys ever? Below, you can see a wooden puzzle made by a Belgian toy manufacturer called Dubreucq. This was available in Belgian stores in 1943, two years after the book *The Crab with the Golden Claws* was first published.

Once upon a time...

The Crab with the Golden Claws has inspired more than toys and games. Part of the story has been used by Steven Spielberg and Peter Jackson to create a Tintin movie. As a matter of fact, the very first film ever made about Tintin was also based on this story.

In 1946, a Belgian puppet-maker named Claude Misonne directed a stop-motion animated film *The Crab with the Golden Claws* (released in 1947) using puppets. You can see an image from the film on the right, and below you can see a drawing that Hergé created to advertise the film.

Tintin and Captain Haddock set off into the desert. Let's join them and **Explore and Discover!**

EXPLORE AND DISCOVER

Trapped in "the land of thirst," Tintin, Captain Haddock and Snowy wander in the blistering heat. There is nothing but sand on the horizon. Some camel bones give an ominous clue to their location: the largest desert in the world, the Sahara.

THE SAHARA DESERT

★ The Sahara Desert is almost as large as the United States! It covers 3,630,000 square miles, reaching across most of North Africa.

★ Much of the land of Morocco, Tunisia, Chad, Algeria, Egypt, Mali, Niger, Sudan and Libya is covered by the Sahara.

★ Temperatures in the Sahara have reached as high as 136° F (57.7° C).

★ Most of the desert is extremely dry, and even the relatively wet parts can go for years without rain.

★ In 1922 a team of explorers led by Citroën car company director Georges-Marie Haardt (a naturalized Frenchman with Belgian parents) set off to cross the Sahara Desert by car. They used special Citroën-manufactured cars with wheels at the front and rubber tracks (a bit like small tank tracks) at the back. The mission was successful and took 20 days to complete!

CAMELS

Just when it looks like all hope is lost, Tintin and Captain Haddock are rescued by men called *méharistes*, who are under the command of Lieutenant Delcourt from the Afghar outpost. The French word *méhariste* refers to
camel cavalry. The French army used camels to patrol the Sahara Desert in
the early 1900s.

Lieutenant Delcourt and his men come to the aid of Tintin and Haddock
once again when they are attacked by bandits! The desert troops then
accompany Tintin and Captain Haddock for the rest of their journey, just to
be on the safe side. They travel in a caravan—a traveling group—of camels.

...THE BEST WAY TO CROSS THE DESERT!

★ There are two types of camels: dromedaries have one hump, while Bactrian camels have two.

★ Domesticated dromedaries are common in North Africa, providing people with transport as well as food and milk.

★ When desert conditions are not too extreme, camels can get enough water from eating green leaves to survive without drinking.

★ Camels can sweat up to 25 percent of their body weight in water without being harmed; more than 15 percent is fatal for most mammals.

★ Camels can go for long periods without drinking—even an entire winter— but when they find water, they can drink up to 50 gallons at once!

★ Contrary to popular belief, camels do not store water in their humps. Instead, they store a reserve of fat in their humps, concentrating it into a single place to prevent it from covering the body and causing overheating.

CAPTAIN HADDOCK

In *The Crab with the Golden Claws*, Hergé introduces the character Captain Haddock, an irascible British sailor who becomes Tintin's friend and traveling companion for life.

At home one evening, Hergé was pondering what last name he should give his new character. He asked his wife, Germaine, what they were having for dinner. Germaine said, "Haddock," and then added, "It's a sad English fish." It was a flash of inspiration for Hergé: he had found the name for his new character!

But the captain still needed a first name. Look at the lists, reproduced on the left, that Hergé drew up while choosing Haddock's first name. Readers didn't learn that the captain's first name is Archibald until the twenty-third Tintin adventure, *Tintin and the Picaros* (1976).

INSPIRATION

Edgar Pierre Jacobs was Hergé's assistant and helped him redraw and color the early black-and-white Tintin books in the 1940s (see the Young Readers Edition of *Cigars of the Pharaoh*). Hergé once said that Captain Haddock was like Jacobs: "He is gruff, makes expansive gestures and sometimes has accidents!"

As the adventures go on, it becomes clear that, when not in his blue sailor sweater, Captain Haddock likes to dress in a smart, British style. Hergé appreciated English fashion and enjoyed dressing the captain up. Edgar Jacobs liked wearing tweed jackets—very British! When he created his own comic strip series starring two British heroes, Blake and Mortimer (Mortimer is shown below), Jacobs also enjoyed drawing their clothes!

Philip Mortimer   Edgar Pierre Jacobs   Hergé   Captain Haddock

© Le Mystère de la grande pyramide T1,
Editions BLAKE & MORTIMER - STUDIO JACOBS
(DARGAUD-LOMBARD S.A.) 1986 by E.P. Jacobs

AN AMUSING EDUCATION

Readers of Tintin are treated to a highly unusual education. This is thanks to Captain Haddock, who has, it first appears, a problem with bad language. It quickly becomes apparent, however, that the words he uses are elevated far above ordinary rude insults!

Apparently Hergé got the idea for Captain Haddock's illuminating outbursts when he heard a man arguing with a shopkeeper. Tempers flared, and all of a sudden, the shopkeeper accused his customer of being a "Four Powers Pact," in reference to a peace treaty signed between Britain, France, Germany and Italy in 1933. The random insult stunned his opponent into defeat!

Hergé used dictionaries to find interesting and unusual words for the captain, while the English translators of Tintin mainly used a thesaurus—a book that lists words of similar meaning together—and two books called *Prehistoric Life* and *Reptiles, Mammals and Fishes of the World*.

Tintin fans have counted over two hundred words used by Captain Haddock when he is angry. Below you can learn what some of them mean!

CAPTAIN HADDOCK'S VOCABULARY

★ Troglodyte: a caveman.
★ Iconoclast: someone who destroys religious symbols.
★ Ectoplasm: a spooky substance created by mediums communicating with ghosts.
★ Bashi-bazouk: a Turkish mercenary soldier.
★ Parasite: an organism that lives on another organism.
★ Heretic: someone who goes against established religious beliefs.
★ Gyroscope: a spinning device used to establish orientation.
★ Anthracite: a shiny, hard type of coal.
★ Anthropithecus: an ape or chimpanzee.
★ Ostrogoth: a Germanic tribe that set up a kingdom in Italy in the fifth century.

Four pages are just not enough to introduce Captain Haddock properly. The best way to find out more about the rough and blustery, but faithful and kindhearted, captain is to read more Tintin adventures!

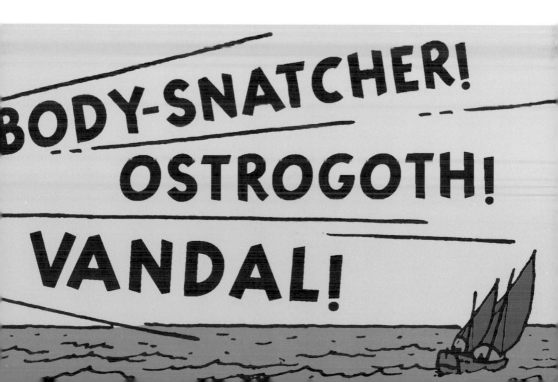

A PHILOSOPHER...

After the camel caravan arrives in the fictional Moroccan port city of Bagghar (from *bagarre*, which means "a fight" in French) Captain Haddock is kidnapped. Tintin dresses up in disguise and sets out to rescue his friend.

While hiding in a cellar, Tintin gives Snowy a quick history lesson. But who was Diogenes?

As for me, Snowy, I'm like old Diogenes, seeking a man! You've never heard of Diogenes! . . . He was a philosopher in ancient Greece, and he lived in a barrel . . .

Diogenes, by Jean-Léon Gérôme (1824–1904). Diogenes praised dogs for their simple lifestyles.

...LIVING IN A BARREL

★ Diogenes (born around 412 B.C.; died 323 B.C.) was a Greek philosopher. He was one of the founders of the Cynic philosophy.

★ The Cynics thought that the purpose of life was to live simply and to reject the conventional trappings of fame, power and wealth.

★ Diogenes practiced what he preached. When he moved to Athens, the leading city of ancient Greece, he made a virtue out of living a life of poverty.

★ The philosopher really did live in a barrel in the market square and beg for a living.

★ It is said that he walked around with a lamp in the middle of the day, claiming to be looking for an honest man.

★ Diogenes poured scorn on conventionally polite behavior. Like Captain Haddock, he was fond of using colorful language!

★ Diogenes was fearless. The picture below shows the moment when Diogenes met the most powerful man in the world, Alexander the Great. When the great Greek king asked the philosopher if there was anything he could do for him, Diogenes replied: "Yes. Can you get out of my sunlight?"

Diogenes and Alexander,
by Lovis Corinth (1858–1925).

THE BEST BONE EVER!

Once Tintin rescues Captain Haddock, it is not long before the heroes manage to crack the smuggling ring of the Crab with the Golden Claws. When they arrive home, Tintin and Snowy are famous once again, as we can see when a surprise comes in the mail!

TINTIN'S GRAND ADVENTURE

The Crab with the Golden Claws was the last Tintin story to be originally drawn in black and white. From this point onward, every Tintin adventure was created in the 62-page color format we know today. The most significant thing about the story, however, is usually considered to be the introduction of Captain Haddock. From now on, Tintin has a human companion for his adventures, in addition to his dog, Snowy!

Trivia: *The Crab with the Golden Claws*

This story features in The Simpsons. When Bart insults Belgium, Marge threatens to take his Tintin books away. Bart clutches a copy of Crab close to his chest, promising he'll be good!

One of Hergé's two favorite drawings from Tintin is in Red Rackham's Treasure. The other one is in this adventure (page 38, panel A2). Hergé said that it looked like a sequence showing a single person getting up and running away.

With almost no exceptions, Captain Haddock is called Captain Haddock in every different translation of Tintin. But in the Afrikaans language (spoken in South Africa), he is called Captain Sardine!

Diogenes is credited with the first-ever use of the word "cosmopolitan." When asked where he came from, the philosopher answered, "I am a world citizen" (kosmopolitês in Greek).

The original cover for *The Crab with the Golden Claws* (1941)

GO ON MORE ADVENTURES WITH TINTIN!

THE SECRET OF THE UNICORN

RED RACKHAM'S TREASURE

CIGARS OF THE PHARAOH

THE BLUE LOTUS

TINTIN IN AMERICA

THE BROKEN EAR

THE BLACK ISLAND

KING OTTOKAR'S SCEPTRE

THE CRAB WITH THE GOLDEN CLAWS

THE SHOOTING STAR

ALSO AVAILABLE